Corey R. Tabor

FOX
and the
BIKE RIDE

photography by Frog

BALZER + BRAY
An Imprint of HarperCollinsPublishers

HarperCollins
PUBLISHERS
Since 1817

Balzer + Bray is an imprint of HarperCollins Publishers.

Fox and the Bike Ride
Copyright © 2017 by Corey R. Tabor
All rights reserved. Manufactured in China.

Library of Congress Control Number: 2016952692
ISBN 978-0-06-239875-8

The artist used pencil, watercolor, colored pencil, and ink, assembled digitally,
to create the illustrations for this book.
Typography by Dana Fritts
Title hand lettering by Alexandra Snowdon
17 18 19 20 21   SCP   10 9 8 7 6 5 4 3 2 1
❖
First Edition

For Mom and Dad

It was the morning of the bike ride—the
Annual Tour de Tip-Top, Slow-and-Steady,
There-and-Back bike ride (plus snacks).

The other animals were *very* excited.

Fox was not.

Every year it was the same thing.
They rode up the tallest hill, ate
snacks at the tip-top, and rode right
back home again.

They saw
the clouds.

They saw
the ocean.

Would you
look at that!

Ooh!
Ah!

Fox wanted adventure.
Fox wanted action-adventure.
Fox wanted danger-action-adventure.
Fox wanted high-flying, deep-sea-diving,
danger-action-adventure . . . on a bike.

(Oh, and snacks. Fox wanted those too.)

"Aha," said Fox. "I know just the thing. . . ."

After breakfast it was time to prepare for
the bike ride.

Rabbit was in charge of plotting the course.
Frog was in charge of photography.
Turtle was in charge of safety.

Elephant was in charge of carrying stuff. (She had the biggest backpack.) She was also in charge of team spirit. (She had the biggest heart.)

Bear was in charge of snacks.

And Fox? Well, Fox was in charge of the bikes.

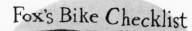

Fox's Bike Checklist

1. wheels
2. frame
3. gears + pedals + seats
4. chain
5. handlebars
6. secret red button (shh)

There. Everything was ready.

Let the bike ride begin!

poof

The animals went over

and over

and over . . .

. . . and up.

They pedaled to the tip-top of the tallest
hill, where they always stopped for snacks.
But they did not stop, because they *could*
not stop, because . . .

Fox forgot the brakes.

chunk

The animals saw the clouds.

"Would you look at that!" said Turtle.

They saw the tall, tall trees.
"Bravo!" said Rabbit.
Bear was speechless.

They saw the ocean.
"Ooh!" said Frog.
"Ah!" said Elephant.
"Bwaack!" said Chicken.

crack

Goldfish!

And they forgot all about being mad at Fox. (Except for Elephant, who never forgot but was quick to forgive.)

"Gurgle glub burble," said the animals, which probably means, "Best bike ride ever!"

Bwaack?

Or maybe it means,

"SHAAAARKS!"

screech

Suddenly, it was all danger and action and adventure!

FLASH

Goldfish!

And snacks. Finally, it was snacks.
(Well, not for Fox. His snack was
nowhere to be found.)

"Mrrm mr-hmm mmr-hm!" said
the animals, which almost certainly
means, "Best bike ride ever!"

Bwaack?

It was the evening of the bike ride—the First Annual Tour de Tip-Top, High-Flying, Deep-Sea-Diving, Danger-Action-Adventure bike ride.

The other animals were plumb full and *very* sleepy.

Fox was not.